Moving Day

Originally published under the title *The Good-by Day.*

By Leone Castell Anderson
Illustrated by Eugenie

A GOLDEN BOOK • NEW YORK

Western Publishing Company, Inc., Racine, Wisconsin

Copyright © 1984 by Leone Castell Anderson. Illustrations copyright © 1984 by Eugenie Fernandes. All rights reserved. Printed in the U.S.A. by Western Publishing Company, Inc. No part of this book may be reproduced or copied in any form without written permission from the publisher. GOLDEN®, GOLDEN & DESIGN®, A GOLDEN BOOK®, and A LITTLE GOLDEN BOOK® are trademarks of Western Publishing Company, Inc. Library of Congress Catalog Card Number: 83-80025 ISBN 0-307-02090-8/ ISBN 0-307-60236-2 (lib. bdg.)   D E F G H I J

Jennifer and Zaneed were best friends. They walked to school together. They took turns pushing each other on the swings. They made mud pies and sand castles in the big sandbox.

And they had their own special joke
that no one else knew about.
Jennifer loved her friend.

One day Jennifer's mother had some news for her. "Daddy and I have found wonderful new jobs in another town," she said. "We are all going to move soon. We'll live in a new house with a big back yard."

"Can Zaneed come too?" asked Jennifer.

"No," said her mother. "Zaneed will stay here with her family. But you'll make new friends when we move."

Jennifer watched her mother and father pack things into boxes. She even helped pack some of her toys.

Soon it was moving day. Jennifer sat on the porch and watched the movers carry furniture out to the big van.

She felt sad. She didn't want to move away. She didn't want to say good-by to Zaneed.

Zaneed came running up the path. "Hi," she said. "Let's go swing."

"I don't want to," said Jennifer.

"Then let's go make mud pies," said Zaneed.

"No," said Jennifer. "I don't feel like it."

"Okay," said Zaneed, smiling. "I guess you're too little to do anything, because you only come up to here!" She held her hand up to her eyebrows.

"I am not too little!" said Jennifer. "I come up to here." She put her hand on top of her head. But she was thinking so hard about leaving that she didn't laugh at their special joke.

Just then Jennifer's father called them inside. When they were in the kitchen, he took a coconut out of a bag. "This is for you," he told the girls.

Zaneed laughed when she saw the coconut. "It's hairy," she said. She laughed even more when Jennifer's father cracked it open with a hammer and the coconut milk dribbled onto the table.

Jennifer began to laugh too. Zaneed always made things seem funny.

Jennifer's father took pictures of the girls as they ate the coconut meat and sipped the milk. "Did you have coconuts where you used to live?" he asked Zaneed.

"I don't remember," she replied. "I wasn't big enough. I only came up to here." She put her hand just above the floor.

She and Jennifer giggled at their special joke. Jennifer's father took pictures of them laughing together.

The movers came into the kitchen. They carried out the chairs.

Suddenly Jennifer burst into tears and ran outside.

Her father followed her. He swung her up into his arms.

"I don't want to move," Jennifer cried. She put her head on his shoulder.

"But Mommy and I told you why we have to leave," he said.

"I don't care!" said Jennifer. "I don't want to move away from Zaneed."

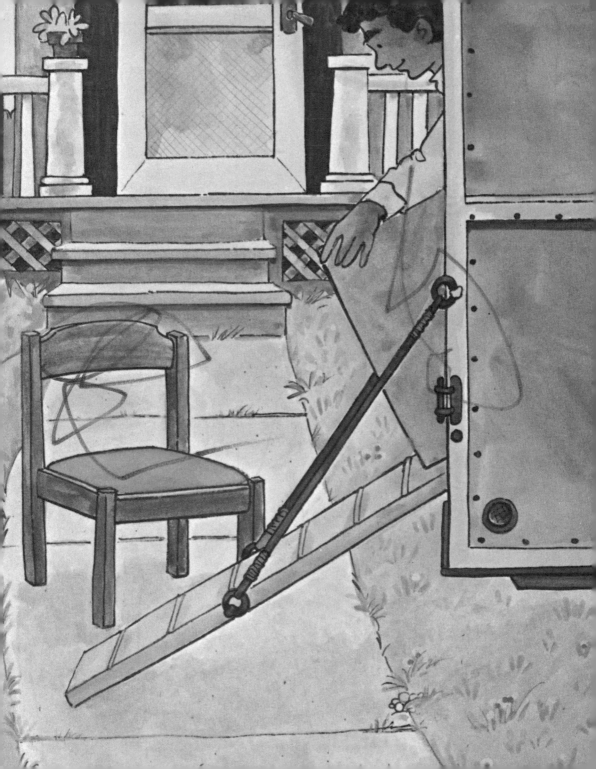

Jennifer's father took her back inside.

Zaneed didn't say anything, but her eyes were sad.

"Look," said Jennifer's father. "There are pictures of both of you inside this camera. I'll make copies of the pictures for you. Then you can see each other whenever you want to."

"But that's not the same as being together," said Jennifer.

"I know," said her father. "But the pictures will help you remember how much fun you had together. And you can talk on the telephone and write letters to each other."

He knelt down beside them. "Sometimes you'll even be able to visit each other. Then you'll see how much you've each been growing."

Zaneed grinned. "Maybe next time I see you," she said to Jennifer, "you'll come up to here." She put her hand on top of her head.

Jennifer smiled. Their special joke made her feel a little better.

"It's time to leave," said Jennifer's father. "We're going to have to say good-by."

Jennifer's eyes filled with tears again.

Her father put his arm around her. "Saying good-by doesn't mean you aren't ever going to say hello again," he said. "Good-by is just a sort of backward hello."

Zaneed nodded. She walked toward the door. Suddenly she stopped. She took three steps backward. "Hello!" she called. Then she turned around. She was laughing.

Jennifer laughed too. Zaneed could always make things seem funny—even having to say good-by.

Jennifer loved her friend.